The original American edition of this book was published 1963.

© for the French edition: 2018, Le Lièvre de Mars Varennes, Québec, Canada.
© for the new English edition: 2020, Prestel Verlag Munich · London · New York
A member of Verlagsgruppe Random House GmbH
Neumarkter Strasse 28 · 81673 Munich
This edition was published by arrangement with The Picture Book Agency, France.
All rights reserved.

In respect to links in the book, the Publisher expressly notes that no illegal content was discernible on the linked sites at the time the links were created. The Publisher has no influence at all over the current and future design, content or authorship of the linked sites. For this reason the Publisher expressly disassociates itself from all content on linked sites that has been altered since the link was created and assumes no liability for such content.

Library of Congress Control Number: 2019938587
A CIP catalogue record for this book is available from the British Library.

Proofreading: John Son
Project Management: Melanie Schöni
Production management and typesetting: Susanne Hermann
Printing and binding: DZS Grafik d.o.o.
Paper: Tauro Offset

FSC
www.fsc.org
MIX
Paper from responsible sources
FSC® C106600

Verlagsgruppe Random House FSC® N001967

Printed in Slovenia

ISBN 978-3-7913-7419-2
www.prestel.com

That's Good, That's Bad

Text by
JOAN M. LEXAU

Illustrations by
ALIKI

Prestel
Munich · London · New York

Boy was just sitting on a rock in the jungle when along came Tiger.
"Run," said Tiger. "And I will run after you. And I will catch you."

"And I will eat you, Boy, so run from me." Boy just sat there and looked at Tiger.
"Eat me then," said Boy. "I have no more run in me."

"Don't be silly," said Tiger. "Why can't you run?
Tell me that and THEN I will eat you."

"Well, it's like this," said Boy. "I was walking, just walking in the jungle when bump ..."

"... I bumped into Rhino. Or Rhino bumped into me. I was willing to forget it, but not Rhino. He got mad, so I ran away from there fast."

"That's good," said Tiger.

"I ran and I ran and I ran and I ran," said Boy. "All the way, there was Rhino
running after me. He can't see well, but he can run fast."

"That's bad," said Tiger.

"So, there we were running along," said Boy. "Then I saw a low tree.
I got up into it. Rhino was running so fast, he went right by."

"That's good," said Tiger.

"Yes, but Rhino came back looking for me," said Boy. "Oh, was he mad!"

"That's bad," said Tiger.

"I got down and picked up a stone and threw it at Rhino," said Boy.

"Good," said Tiger. "Good for you."

"It didn't hit him," said Boy.

"That's bad," said Tiger.

"I ran again – not very fast. I was getting tired, but so was Rhino," said Boy.

"That's good," said Tiger.

"I ran and I ran and I ran with Rhino running right after me. And then I fell," said Boy.

"My, that is bad," said Tiger.

"But Rhino was running so fast, he went right over me," said Boy.

"That's good," said Tiger.

"As soon as I got up, there was Rhino, back again," said Boy.

"That's bad," said Tiger.

"I saw a vine on a tree, so I swung on it right over the river," said Boy.

"That's good," said Tiger.

"And there on the other side of the river was Crocodile," said Boy.

"That's bad," said Tiger.

"So I swung back to the other side again," said Boy. "I jumped off the vine."

"That's good," said Tiger.

"I didn't see Rhino – not right away, that is," said Boy.
"Then I saw I was sitting on his back!"

"That's terrible!" said Tiger.

"So I jumped off and ran in back of a tree. I picked up a stone and threw it as far as I could," said Boy. "You know Rhino can't see well. He heard the stone and went running after it."

"That's good," said Tiger. "Then you ran and you got away from Rhino?"
"Oh, no," said Boy. "I was too tired to run away. I just sat here."

"But ..." said Tiger. "And here comes Rhino now," said Boy.
He got in back of the rock and said, "Here I am, Rhino, over here!"

"Help! This is bad!" said Tiger as Rhino went after him.

"Oh, no, it's good. It's very, very good," said Boy.
He wasn't tired anymore, so he ran along home as fast as he could.

END

ABOUT THIS BOOK

To avoid being eaten by Tiger, Boy tells a long and winding tale about being chased by Rhino. The story is similar to the *Arabian Nights*, the classic collection of Middle Eastern folktales in which a virgin named Scheherazade tells the king an exciting story night after night to keep herself alive. After a thousand and one nights of marvelous tales, the king realizes he has fallen in love with Scheherazade and spares her life.

The original edition of this picture book first appeared in 1962 as part of the Weekly Reader Children's Book Club collection of the American publisher The Dial Press. Aliki, the book's illustrator, says that the greatest challenge with this story was to make the confrontation between Tiger and Boy as straightforward and simple as possible, while still depicting the story of the pursuit in the background.

In the original publication, Aliki used offset processing techniques to apply specific color prints onto acetate film to separate the paints and ensure they were as bright as the original prints. For this current edition of the book, the illustrations were digitized and retouched on the basis of a 1963 copy.

Sketches by Aliki from 1963

ABOUT THE AUTHORS

JOAN M. LEXAU used to work for the publisher Harper & Row before taking up writing. She is the author of some 50 books for children and teenagers, winning awards for *Striped Ice Cream, The Trouble with Terry, Go Away, Dog,* and many other titles. Some of her works have also appeared under the name Joan L. Nodset. Her books are driven by a deep appreciation for how children creatively face the challenges of life and our environment. Joan still lives in her home town of Saint Paul, Minnesota.

Aliki Liacouras Brandenberg, aka **ALIKI**, is an American author and illustrator of children's and teen books. Born in 1929, she still works at her art every day and also illustrates other author's books, including those by her husband, Franz Brandenberg. Aliki once stated that she invents stories to express herself, that she writes documentaries to satisfy her curiosity, and that she draws so as to be able to relax. In 1991, she was given the Pennsylvania School Librarians Association Award. She lives with her husband in London, England.